Pete the Cat

Giant Sticker Book

by
James Dean

Cool!

HARPER FESTIVAL
An Imprint of HarperCollinsPublishers

Star Shine

Pete the Cat sings "Twinkle, Twinkle, Little Star." Help him light up the sky with even more stars. Then use the lines to help some of the stars shine bright.

Pete's Bedtime Story

Pete loves his bedtime story, but he's ready for some new ones before he goes to sleep. And he likes it when the stories are all about *him!* Put a sticker on each page and then tell Pete a story about it.

Pete Rocks Out

Pete loves to make music. Help him fill the page with musical notes. Then sing a song out loud.

Starry Summer Night

Decorate Pete's sky.

Pete Says...

Help Pete say all the important things he has to say.

Sticky Shapes

Match the shape stickers to the pictures.

Pete's Sneakers

Before he stepped in strawberries, blueberries, and mud, Pete's sneakers were totally white!

Decorate Pete's white shoes however you like.

Make a Match!

Two shoes make a pair.
Add the stickers so each
shoe has a match.

Here are Pete's **white** shoes.

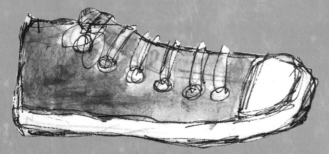

Here are Pete's **blue** shoes.

Here are Pete's **red** shoes.

Here are Pete's **brown** shoes.

E-I-E-I-O

Add all the animals that Pete sings about in "Old MacDonald Had a Farm."

Add the E-I-E-I-O letter stickers and some musical notes. Then sing the song.

Lunchtime

Pete is hungry. He is ready to eat. Give him some yummy food for a groovy lunch. Which is your favorite?

Pete's Phone

Pete wants to call his friends.
Add his friends to the picture.

What do you think he wants
to say to them? What does
each friend say to Pete?

Pete the Reader

What do you think Pete might like to read about?
Add it to Pete's library.

What would you like to read about?

Ready for School

Pete is ready for school.
Share your favorite letters and numbers.

Pete's Masterpiece

Pete is making a huge painting of his goldfish, Goldie. But he needs his art supplies to finish. Add them. Then finish coloring in his masterpiece.

Baseball Practice

Pete and his team practice before the big game.
Add the bats and balls so they can play.

Baseball Words

Pete can read important baseball words like *mitt*, *bat*, *ball*, and *team*.

Put a sticker word on each picture to tell what it is.

C-A-T Spells Cat

Add the letters C, A, and T onto Pete's favorite shirt. Then trace the letters to practice writing the word cat. Cool!

CAT
CAT
CAT
CAT
CAT
CAT
CAT

Pete's Photo Album

Help Pete make a photo album showing his friends and family.

Groovy Buttons

Pete is playing with his groovy buttons. Look at each pattern he made.

What comes next in each pattern?

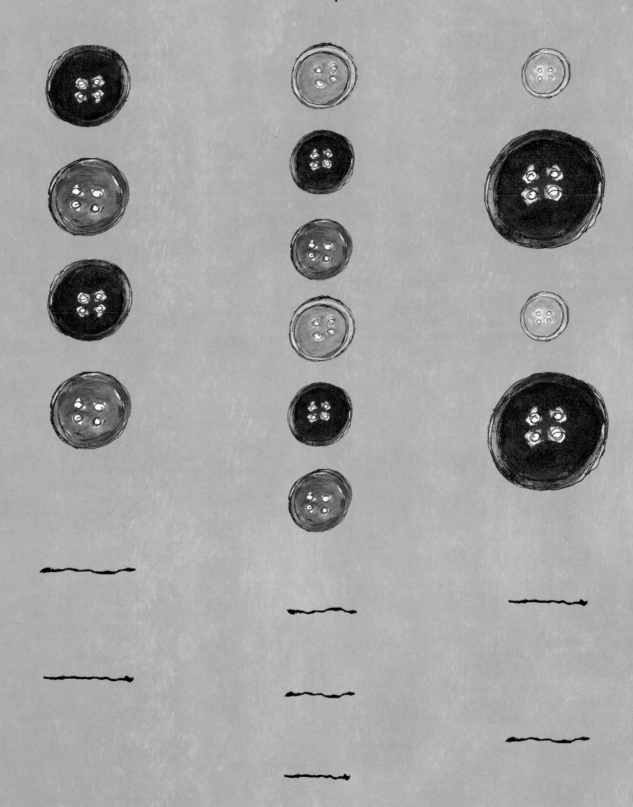

The New Guy

Gus the Platypus is new to the neighborhood.
Help him make some new friends.

Buttoned Up

Put the right number of buttons on Pete's shirts.

Tiny Pattern Pals

Look at each pattern Pete's teeny tiny friends made. What comes next in each pattern?

Pete's Magic Sunglasses

Pete's magic sunglasses show him how to look for the good in every day.

Add stickers to show all the good things he sees.

Pete the Bus Driver

Pete is driving the bus. Give him the things he needs.

Then sing "The Wheels on the Bus" out loud!

Color Combinations

Teach Pete how to mix paint to make new colors.

Pete's Dreams

Pete woke up this morning and remembered some weird dreams he had last night. Put the dream stickers around his bed. Then tell a story about each one. Start with "Pete dreamed that . . ."

Shopping List

Pete is going to help his mom go shopping. They have a list. Add stickers to show how many of each thing they need.

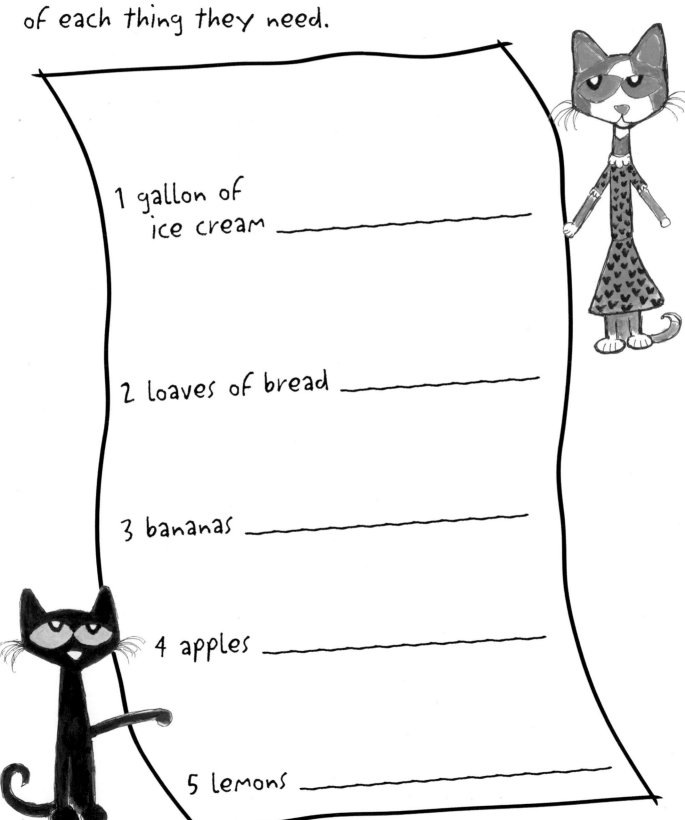

1 gallon of
  ice cream _____

2 loaves of bread _____

3 bananas _____

4 apples _____

5 lemons _____

Good Buddies

Pete the Cat knows how to be a good friend.
Put the stickers on the right shapes to show what
a good buddy does.

Shares

Helps you learn something new

Listens to you when you are talking

Makes you laugh

Pete's Color Match

Show the red, yellow, and blue things in Pete's world. Sort the stickers by color.

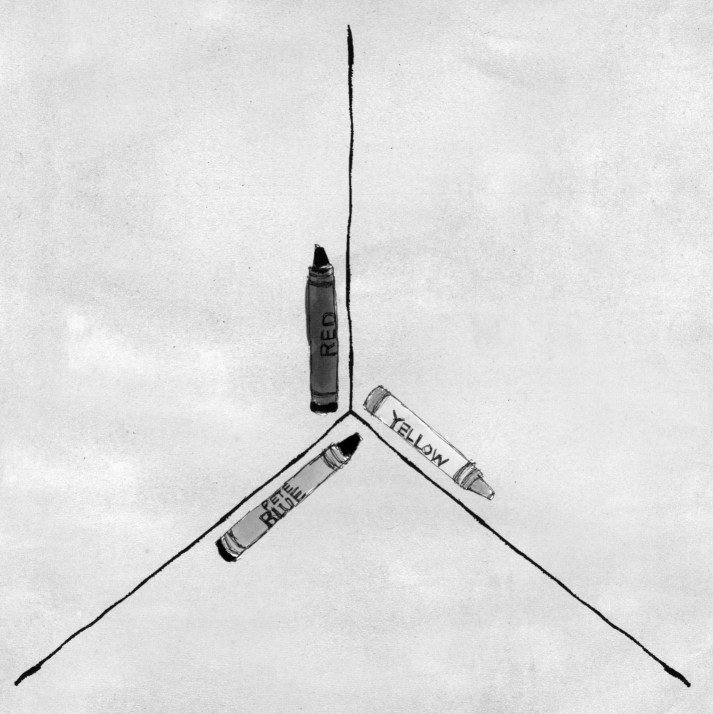

Frog & Dog Tic-Tac-Toe

Play with a friend. Instead of Xs and Os, use frogs and dogs.

Through Pete's Telescope

What does Pete see through his telescope?

Groovy Scoops

Add scoops of ice cream to help Pete's mom make him a tall, groovy ice-cream cone.

Old MacDonald's Farm

Put the baby animals with their parents.

Pete's Fabulous Fruit Salad

Want to learn how to make Pete's favorite fruit salad?
Add the stickers to complete the recipe.

One
squirt of

One

One

One

Juice
of one

A handful of

One cut-up slice
of

Pete at the Beach

What does Pete see at the beach?

Pete's Bedtime Story

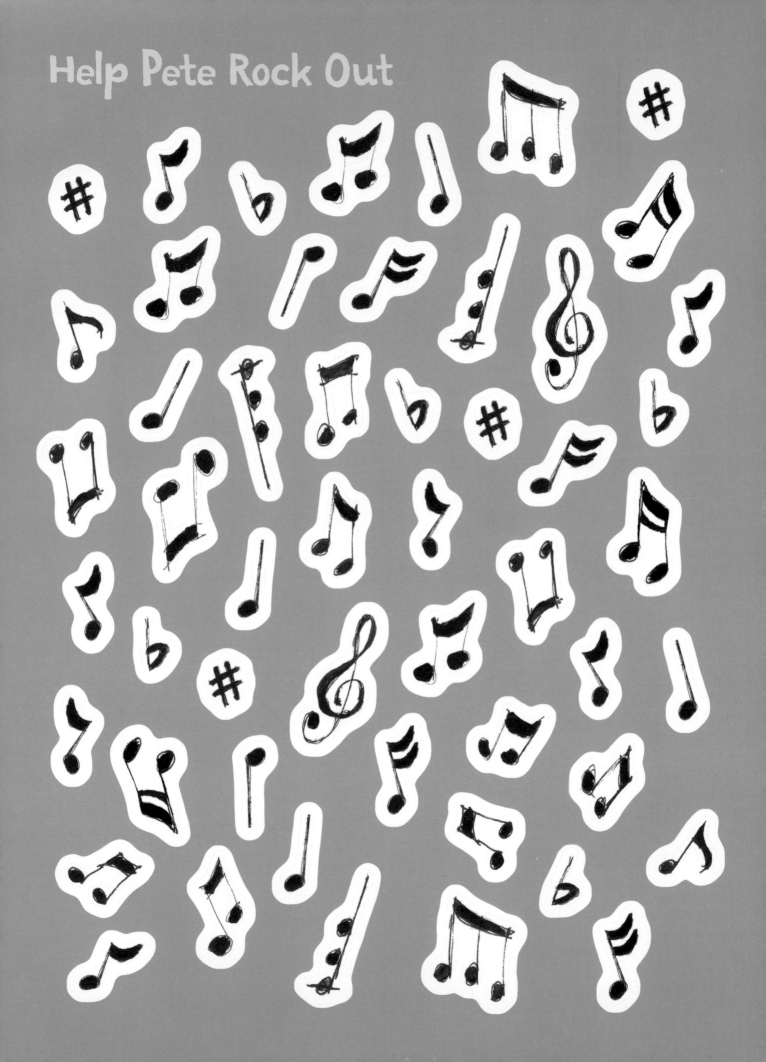

Help Pete Rock Out

Starry Summer Night

Pete Says...

Sticky Shapes

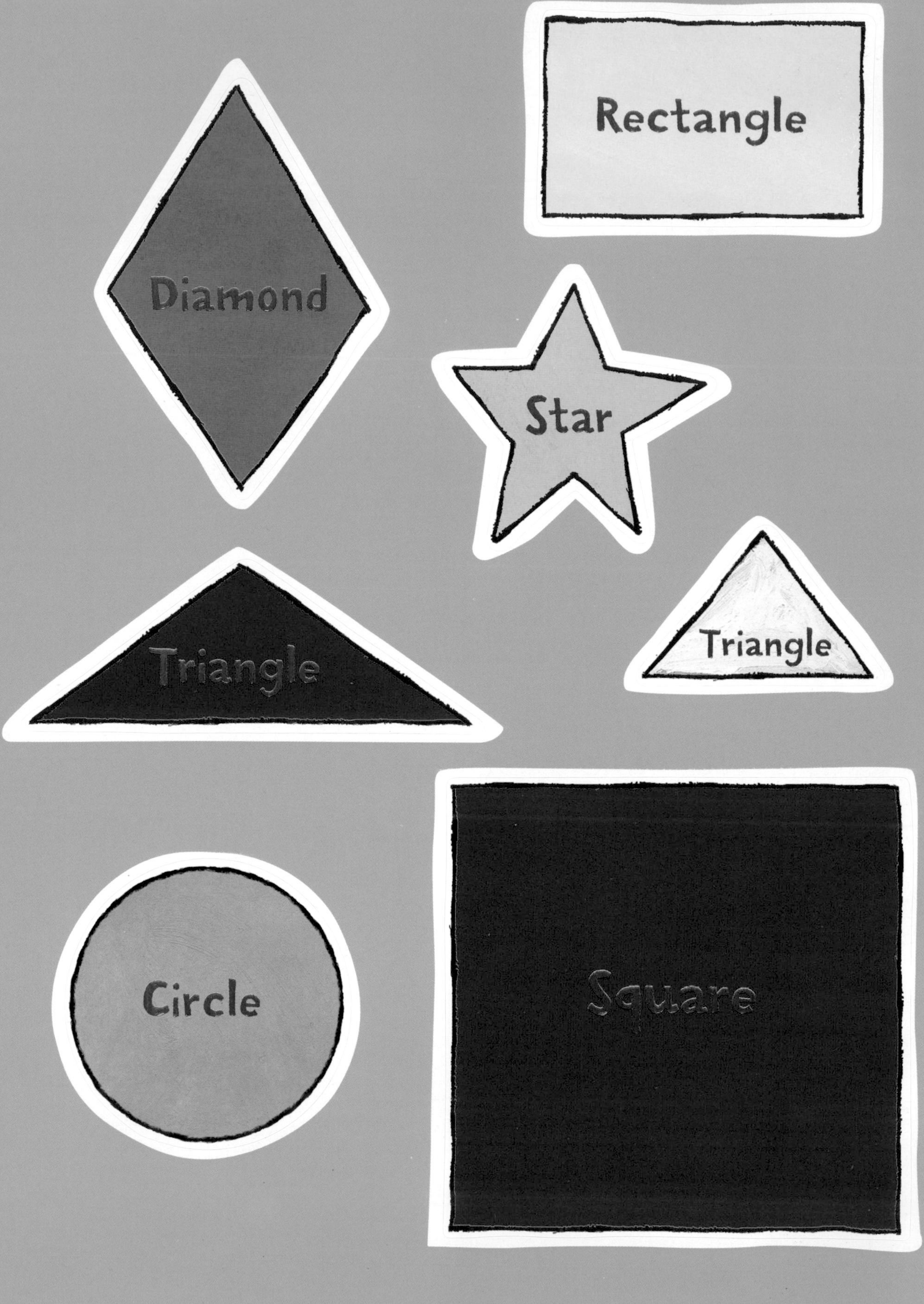

Diamond

Rectangle

Star

Triangle

Triangle

Circle

Square

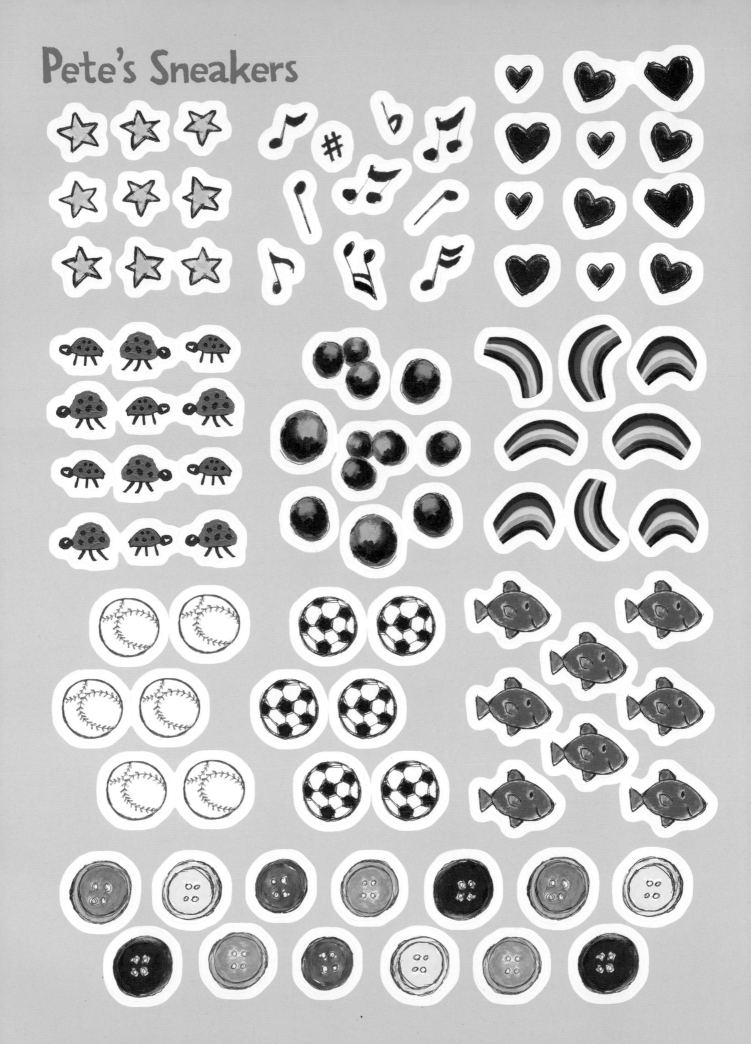

Pete's Sneakers

Make a Match!

white

blue

red

brown

Lunchtime

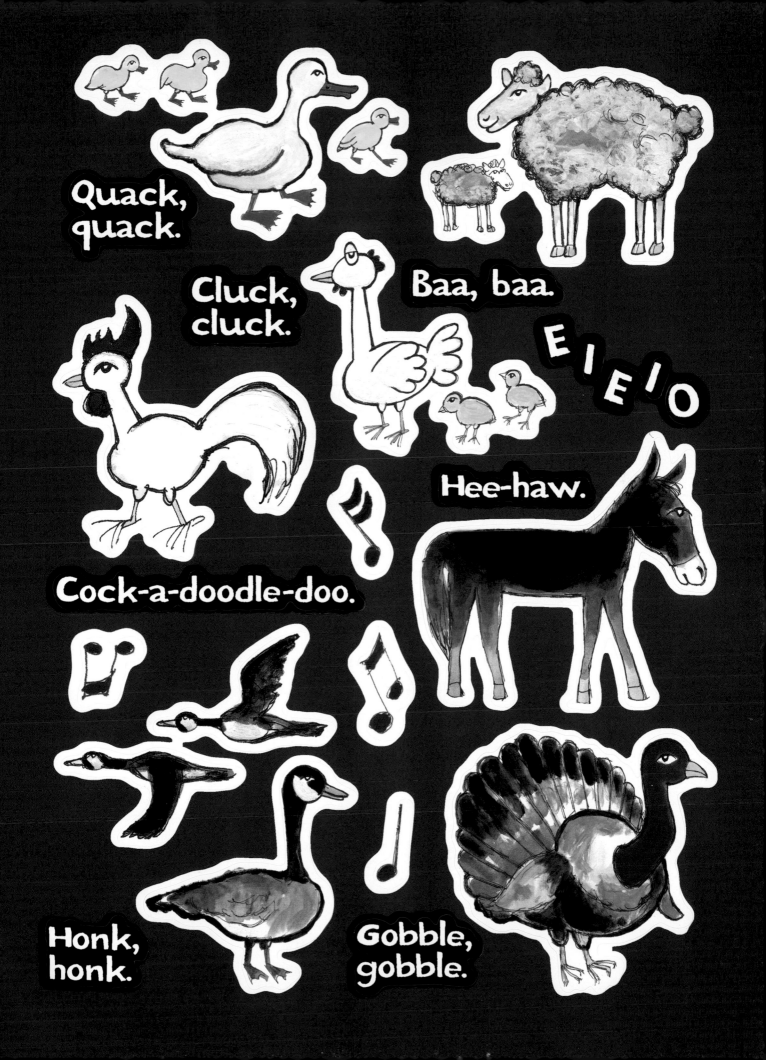

Pete's Phone

Pete the Reader

Ready for School

A B C D E F G
H I J K L M N
O P Q R S T U
V W X Y Z + −
= 0 1 2 3 4
5 6 7 8 9 10

Pete's Masterpiece

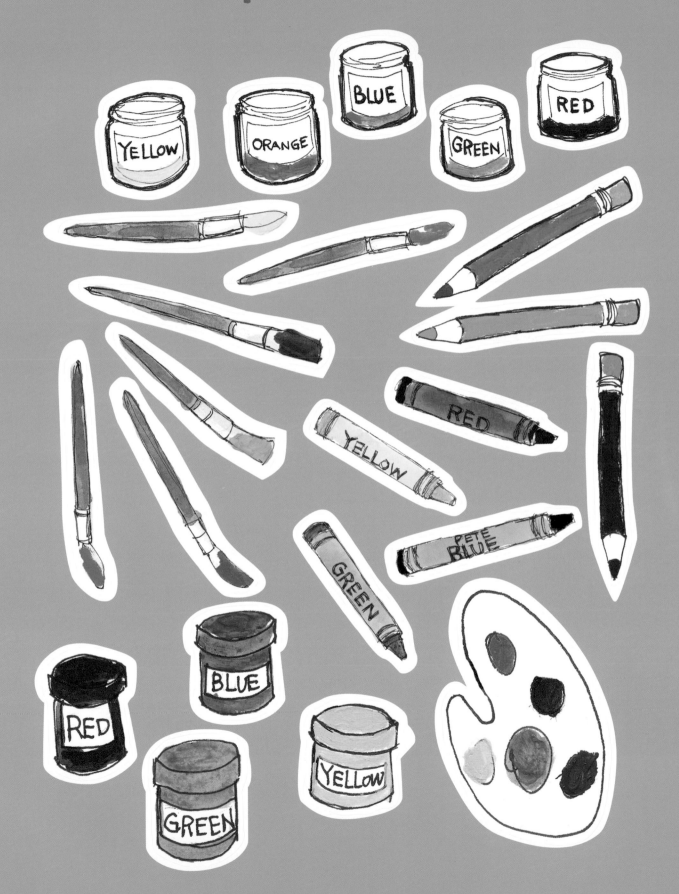

Baseball Practice

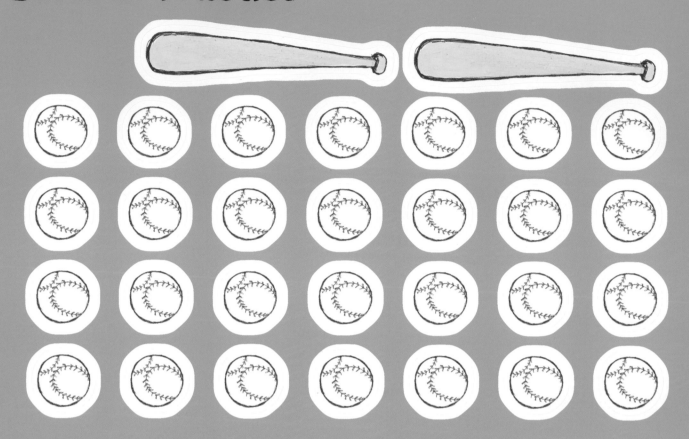

Baseball Words

team **mitt**

C-A-T Spells Cat

CAT **ball**

bat

Pete's Photo Album

Gus

Turtle

Alligator

Marty

Emma

Squirrel

Goldie

Grumpy Toad

Owl

Bob

Callie

Mom

Coach

Grandma

Groovy Buttons

Buttoned Up

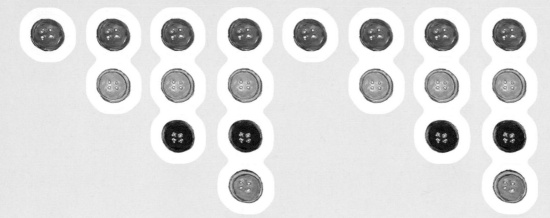

Tiny Pattern Pals

Pete's Magic Sunglasses

Pete's Buddies

The sun is shining. The sky is bright.

Pete's Favorite Things

Pete's Family

Pete the Bus Driver

Passengers

BUS STOP

Driver's License

DRIVER'S LICENSE
PETE the cat
123 CATALINA PKWY
CAT CITY, USA

HEIGHT   1-06
WEIGHT   12 LBS
BIRTH DATE   1999
FUR COLOR   BLUE
CLASS   BIG TRUCKS
RESTRICTIONS   NONE

Beep, beep, beep.

Signs

STOP

Wheels

Zoom, zoom, zoom.

BUS

Flashers

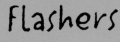

Motor

Tools

Battery

Headlights

Color Combinations

ORANGE GREEN PURPLE

Shopping List

ICE CREAM

Pete's Dreams

Good Buddies

Frog & Dog Tic-Tac-Toe

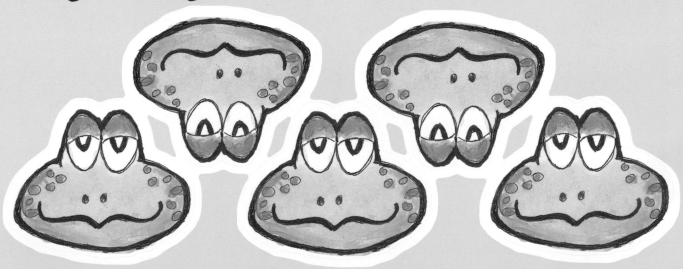

Through Pete's Telescope

Frog & Dog Tic-Tac-Toe

Pete's Color Match

Groovy Scoops

Old MacDonald's Farm

Pete's Fabulous Fruit Salad

Whipped
Cream

Apple

Lemon

Orange

Blueberries

Banana

Watermelon

Pete at the Beach

When I Grow Up

coach

rock star

astronaut

cowboy

2+2=4

teacher

bus driver

BUS

artist